WITHDRAWN

Dear Parent:
Your child's love of reading starts here!

Every child learns to read in a different way and at his or her own speed. Some go back and forth between reading levels and read favorite books again and again. Others read through each level in order. You can help your young reader improve and become more confident by encouraging his or her own interests and abilities. From books your child reads with you to the first books he or she reads alone, there are I Can Read Books for every stage of reading:

SHARED READING
Basic language, word repetition, and whimsical illustrations, ideal for sharing with your emergent reader

BEGINNING READING
Short sentences, familiar words, and simple concepts for children eager to read on their own

READING WITH HELP
Engaging stories, longer sentences, and language play for developing readers

READING ALONE
Complex plots, challenging vocabulary, and high-interest topics for the independent reader

ADVANCED READING
Short paragraphs, chapters, and exciting themes for the perfect bridge to chapter books

I Can Read Books have introduced children to the joy of reading since 1957. Featuring award-winning authors and illustrators and a fabulous cast of beloved characters, I Can Read Books set the standard for beginning readers.

A lifetime of discovery begins with the magical words **"I Can Read!"**

*Visit www.icanread.com for information
on enriching your child's reading experience.*

Also available

Dumpy's Apple Shop

Dumpy to the Rescue

Dumpy's Valentine

HarperCollins®, 🚛®, and I Can Read Book® are trademarks of HarperCollins Publishers Inc.

Library of Congress Cataloging-in-Publication Data

Edwards, Julie, date
  Dumpy's extra-busy day / by Julie Andrews Edwards and Emma Walton Hamilton ; illustrated by Tony Walton with Katie Boyd.—1st ed.
    p.   cm. — (An I can read book) (The Julie Andrews collection)
  "Level 1."
  Summary: Can Dumpy the Dump Truck feed the farm animals and move the pigs to their new pen in time to take Charlie to the school bus?
  ISBN-10: 0-06-088576-9 (trade bdg.) — ISBN-13: 978-0-06-088576-2 (trade bdg.)
  ISBN-10: 0-06-088578-5 (pbk.) — ISBN-13: 978-0-06-088578-6 (pbk.)
  [1. Dump trucks—Fiction. 2. Trucks—Fiction. 3. Domestic animals—Fiction.] I. Hamilton, Emma Walton. II. Walton, Tony, date, ill. III. Title. IV. Series. V. Series: The Julie Andrews collection
PZ7.E2562Dwp 2006   2005017798
[E]—dc22   CIP
                                                                  AC

1 2 3 4 5 6 7 8 9 10 ❖   First Edition

Tony Walton and Katie Boyd warmly thank Ruby Randig

Dumpy's
Extra-Busy Day

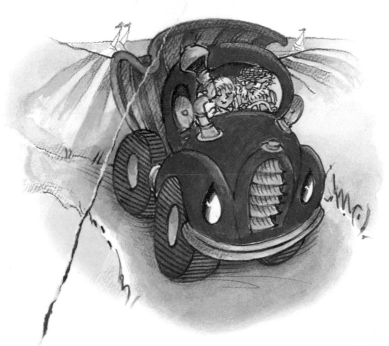

By Julie Andrews Edwards and Emma Walton Hamilton
Illustrated by Tony Walton
with Katie Boyd

HarperCollins Publishers

"Cock-a-Doodle-Doo!"

said the rooster.

4

"Wake up, Dumpy!"

"Brooom! Brooom!" said Dumpy.

He was very sleepy.

"Wake up, Dumpy!" said Pop-Up.

"We have a busy day.

Farmer Barnes has gone to town.

We must do extra work today.

We must plow and mow."

Charlie said,

"And we must feed the animals

and move the pigs.

Then you must take me

to the school bus!"

Now Dumpy was awake.

Could they do all that

and meet the bus on time?

9

"Cluck cluck!"

The hens needed seed.

"Thank you!" said the hens.

"Here are our eggs!"

"Uh-oh!" said Charlie.

"One hen has run away!"

"I can bring her back,"

sang the rooster.

"You go feed the puppies!"

"Woof woof!" said the puppies.

"Thank you!"

"Uh-oh!" said Charlie.

"How can we move all the pigs

to their new pen?"

"We can help!" said the puppies.

"We can herd the pigs into Dumpy."

"Oink oink!" said the pigs.

"Thank you!"

"Uh-oh!" said Pop-Up.

"The gate is stuck!"

"We can help!" said the pigs.

"We can push it shut!"

Nellie the horse needed hay.

"Na-a-y!" she said.

"Thank you!"

"Uh-oh!" said Charlie.

"It's getting late!

Do we have time to plow?"

"I can help!" said Nellie.

"I can pull the plow today!"

"We still need to feed the goats,"
said Pop-Up.

"And mow the grass."

"But we will be late for school!"

said Charlie.

"Maaa!" said the goats.

"No need to mow! We ate the grass.

And the weeds, too!"

"Look, there's the bus!"

said Pop-Up.

"If we hurry, we will not be late."

"Toot! Toot!"

Dumpy called to his friends.

"Thank you for your help!"

"You made all the extra work

seem like fun!"

"Cluck!"

"Woof!"

"Oink!"

"Brooom! Brooom!" said Dumpy.

"That will be *extra* fun

on this extra-busy day!"

"Will you take us for a ride

when our schoolwork is done?"

"Hooray! Here comes Dumpy!"
said the schoolchildren.

"Nay!"

"Maaa!" they called back.

"We had fun, too!"